BEAUTY AND THE BEAST

For my parents,
Merlyn Hutson Heyer and William J. Heyer,
who helped keep the magic alive.

Special thanks to:
Beauty—Lesley Glassford
Merchant—William J. Heyer

Published by Ideals Children's Books
An imprint of Hambleton-Hill Publishing, Inc.
Nashville, Tennessee 37218

Printed and bound in the United States of America

Library of Congress Cataloging-in-Publication Data

Heyer, Carol, 1950–
Beauty and the Beast / retold and illustrated by Carol Heyer.
p. cm.
Summary: Through her great capacity to love, a kind and beautiful maid releases a handsome prince from the spell which has made him an ugly beast.
ISBN 0-8249-8359-9 (trade); ISBN 0-8249-8579-6 (paper)
[1. Fairy tales. 2. Folklore—France.] I. Beauty and the beast.
II. Title.
PZ8.H48Be 1989
398.21'0944—dc20
[E] 89-7624
CIP
AC

BEAUTY AND THE BEAST

RETOLD AND ILLUSTRATED BY CAROL HEYER

Ideals Children's Books · Nashville, Tennessee

Once a rich merchant had three daughters. The youngest daughter was especially beautiful and was called "Little Beauty" when she was little. As she grew older, her name was shortened to "Beauty." Her older sisters were very jealous.

But the rich merchant was suddenly reduced to poverty when all of his trading ships were lost at sea. All he had was a small house in the country. Beauty took the bad news well and began learning how to cook and clean, but her sisters refused to help her and made Beauty serve them.

One day the merchant heard that one of his ships had survived the storm.

"My daughters," he said joyfully, "I must go to the port to claim the ship. What trinkets shall I bring you?"

The older sisters begged for gowns, jewels, and other fine things.

"And what do you wish, my Beauty?" the merchant asked his youngest daughter.

"Oh, perhaps a rose," replied Beauty. "They are so lovely and do not grow around here."

When the merchant reached the port, he discovered that all the valuable cargo had been thrown overboard during the storm to lighten the ship. He was as poor as before.

Miserable and weary, the merchant started home. As he passed through a dark forest not far from his cottage, a sudden storm broke. The wind howled and the thunder raged. A brilliant streak of lightning startled his horse and the merchant was thrown from the saddle. Soon he had completely lost his way in the tangle of trees.

Then in the distance, he saw the glimmer of lights and trudged toward them, expecting to find a woodcutter's cottage. As he drew closer, the merchant saw, to his surprise, that the lights came from a magnificent castle.

The merchant knocked at the gates, but no one appeared. He pushed them open and entered the grounds. Climbing the wide steps, he pounded on the door. When no one came, he opened the great doors and entered the castle. He wandered from room to room, but the place seemed abandoned.

The merchant entered the dining hall and found blazing candles and a banquet table set with a hot supper for one. Because he was wet, cold, and very tired and hungry, he sat down. After waiting awhile to see if anyone came, he said very loudly, "The master of this castle is a generous host, and I thank him for his hospitality." With that, he began to eat.

After he had eaten, he was very sleepy. Still sitting at the table, he fell sound asleep.

The merchant awoke late the next morning. Before him was a hot breakfast for one. As he finished eating, he heard the sounds of a horse's neighing. Rushing to the nearest window, he looked out on a courtyard surrounded by roses of all colors. In the middle of the courtyard was a horse. The merchant ran down the stairs and over to the horse. Just as he was about to mount, he remembered the request from Beauty, to bring back a rose.

"Well, at least I can fill one of my daughter's wishes," he said. He reached out and broke the stem of the largest, most beautiful blue rose he had ever seen. As he did, he leaped back in terror at the loud roar he heard, and a huge ugly beast sprang out in front of him.

"Ungrateful man!" roared the creature. "You have eaten my food, warmed yourself by my fire, and planned to take my horse, all of which I freely give you. I saved your life and you repay me by stealing my most prized possession—my rose! You will die for this!"

The merchant fell to his knees. "Please, my lord. Forgive me. I took the rose only to fulfill a promise to my daughter."

"My name is not 'my lord'," said the creature, "but only Beast. If your daughter should choose to die in your place, you will be free. You may return home. But either you or your daughter must return in three months."

The merchant returned home and was still clutching the blue rose as he told his terrifying tale to his daughters.

The two oldest daughters blamed everything on their younger sister. "If you had not asked for a rose," they cried, "our father's life would not now be in danger."

"Our father is not in danger," said Beauty. "At the end of three months, I will go to the beast."

The merchant, of course, would not allow his daughter to suffer for him. But one morning before the end of three months, Beauty slipped out of the house before her father awoke, mounted the horse, and flew to the castle.

Beauty entered the great hall her father had described. As before, there was a fire and a hot supper for one. Beauty sat down and ate.

When she had finished, she heard an awful roar. Beast entered the room and Beauty thought she would faint.

The creature stood before her and said, "Did you come of your own free will?"

"Yes," Beauty said, shaking from fear.

"You are a good daughter," replied the Beast. With that, he turned and left the room.

Beauty began to cry. After a while, she got up, wiped her tears, and wandered through the castle. She came to a doorway over which hung a sign: "Beauty's Room."

Opening the door, she saw that the room was filled with books, a piano, beautiful paintings on the wall, and, in the closet, gowns covered with jewels.

Looking around the room, Beauty saw a card resting on a golden table. It read:

Welcome, Beauty. Banish fear;
You are queen and monarch here.
Speak your wishes, speak your will.
What you ask will be fulfilled.

"Surely Beast would not have done all this if he plans to eat me soon," Beauty said.

That night as Beauty sat on the porch in the evening, she heard Beast coming. "May I join you?" he asked.

"If you wish," replied Beauty.

After a moment, Beast asked, "Do you think I am ugly?"

Beauty, afraid of making him angry, said nothing.

Beast then asked, "Beauty, will you be my wife?"

Beauty, terrified, was quiet for a long time. Finally, trembling, she said, "No, Beast."

Beast sighed and left the porch.

From then on, every evening, Beast would join Beauty and ask the same question. "Beauty, will you marry me?"

And every evening, the answer was the same, "No, Beast."

Beauty spent three months in the castle. Her every wish was granted almost before she wished it. If she wanted music, it began. If she thought about pretty flowers, they appeared; and every evening, she talked with Beast. She began to look forward to his company.

One evening she said to Beast, "I have come to enjoy our talks and to think of you as a dear friend. But I will never marry you. You have made me very happy here except that I cannot see my father. Sometimes I think I will die if I do not see him again."

Beast could not bear to see Beauty sad, so he told her, "I will send you home to your father, but I will die from loneliness."

"No, Beast," cried Beauty. "I care for you too much to let you die. I will return to you in only one week," she promised.

Beast removed the ruby ring from his finger and placed it in Beauty's palm. "If you only look into this ring and wish, you will return home," he said.

Beauty thanked Beast for his kindness, looked deep into the red of the stone, and wished to be home. When she looked up again, she was in her father's house.

Beauty's father was overjoyed at seeing her alive, for he thought she was dead. But her sisters were only jealous, for Beauty looked happier and more beautiful than before.

She explained to her family that she had to return in one week. Her sisters began to plot and plan.

"If we can keep her home longer than a week," said one sister to the other, "the creature will be so angry when she returns that he will eat her. Then we will be rid of her forever."

When the time came for Beauty to return, the sisters cried and carried on until Beauty agreed to stay one more week. Knowing Beast's kindness, she felt sure he would understand.

On the tenth day at her father's house, Beauty looked into her mirror. She saw the image of Beast; he lay dying in the castle garden. She heard him cry out her name in such pain that she burst into tears.

She rushed to her father and said, "Beast was kind to me. He gave me only happiness and love. In return, I have broken my promise to him."

"I have never been happier than when I was with Beast. Even though his looks are frightening, he is a kind and gentle creature. I would never forgive myself if he died because of me."

Then Beauty took Beast's ring and gazed into its depths. When she looked up again, she was inside the castle keep. At once she began searching for Beast.

Beauty ran to the garden. There she found Beast stretched out beneath an old oak tree. For a moment, she was afraid he was already dead. Beauty knelt beside Beast and gently touched his heart. It was still beating.

"Oh, Beast," she cried. "Can you ever forgive me?"

Beast opened his eyes and looked sadly into hers. "I feared you would never return," he whispered. "Remember, I told you I would surely die without you."

Beauty stroked Beast's face as her eyes filled with tears. "I am here now," she said. "And I will never leave you again."

"It is too late," answered Beast.

"No, do not die," cried Beauty. "I love you. Please do not die."

Suddenly there was a blast of trumpets and the sky exploded with light and color. Beauty turned away for a moment. When she turned back, Beast had disappeared. In his place was a handsome prince.

The young prince said, ''Many years ago a wicked witch condemned me to live as a beast until a beautiful woman fell in love with me. Only then could I be free. Thank you for releasing me from the spell.'' Then the young prince took her hand in his and softly asked, ''Beauty, will you marry me?''

Beauty smiled and whispered, ''Yes.''

Arm in arm, Beauty and the prince strolled back to the castle. There, waiting for them were Beauty's father and her two sisters.

"Beauty," said the prince, "because you looked past the ugliness of Beast and saw kindness, you will now be a princess with a kingdom at your feet."

Turning to Beauty's sisters, the prince continued, "Because of the evil in your hearts, you are banished from my kingdom until you change your selfish ways."

Then Beauty, her father, and the prince returned to the prince's kingdom. His loyal subjects received them with great joy. There Beauty and the prince were married and lived a long and happy life together.

The illustrations in this book were rendered in colored pencils
and using live models.

The text type was set in Baskerville Roman.
The display type was set in Galliard.
Composed by The Font Shop, Nashville, Tennessee.